I would like to thank Emma Dryden and Brenda Bowen for suggesting the idea for this book. As the son of a World War II veteran, my goal in creating this book is to honor the men and women who served in that war as well as in past conflicts in Korea and Vietnam, and who are currently serving in the Gulf and Iraq.

I offer *Alpha Bravo Charlie* to honor not only those who have served and are serving in the military, but also those who have died, making the ultimate sacrifice in the name of freedom. May this book be a tribute to their loved ones.

I also wish to recognize those families that are affected by the long absences of family members serving in the military. Theirs is also a sacrifice.

And, finally, I wish to pay tribute to the media who have risked all, and sometimes lost their lives, to bring us word of what's happening thousands of miles from home.

—C. L. D.

Margaret K. McEldorry Books ■ An imprint of Simon & Schuster Children's Publishing Division ■ 1230 Avenue of the Americas, New York, New York 10020 ■ Copyright © 2005 by Chris L. Demarest ■ All rights reserved, including the right of reproduction in whole or in part in any form. ■ Book design by Abelardo Martínez ■ The text for this book is set in Champion HTF. ■ The illustrations for this book are rendered in pastels. ■ Manufactured in China ■ 10 9 8 7 6 5 4 3 2 1 ■ CIP data for this book is available from the Library of Congress. ■ ISBN 0-689-86928-2

FIRST
EDITION

ALPHA BRAVO CHARLIE
The Military Alphabet

CHRIS L. DEMAREST

Margaret K. McElderry Books
NEW YORK · LONDON · TORONTO · SYDNEY

The Military Alphabet

ALPHA

BRAVO

CHARLIE

DELTA

ECHO

FOXTROT

GOLF

HOTEL

INDIA

JULIET

KILO

LIMA

MIKE

NOVEMBER

OSCAR

PAPA

QUEBEC

ROMEO

SIERRA

TANGO

UNIFORM

VICTOR

WHISKEY

X-RAY

YANKEE

ZULU

Illustration Details

ALPHA: A-4 Skyhawk, Vietnam War ■ BRAVO: U.S. Army, Gulf War ■ CHARLIE: C-130, Iraq War ■ DELTA: USS Cole, DDG67, Gulf War ■ ECHO: U.S. Air Force Special Forces, Afghanistan War ■ FOXTROT: U.S. troops, Iraq War ■ GOLF: River Patrol Boat, Vietnam War ■ HOTEL: Bell UH-1 Iroquois, Vietnam War ■ INDIA: USCG Polar Class icebreaker, contemporary ■ JULIET: Embedded media, Iraq War ■ KILO: German shepherd, Vietnam War ■ LIMA: U.S. Marines landing craft, World War II ■ MIKE: Bell 47 helicopters, Korean War ■ NOVEMBER: U.S. Navy Nuclear Class submarine, contemporary ■ OSCAR: U.S. Marines Harrier Jump Jet, Gulf War ■ PAPA: C-47s, World War II ■ QUEBEC: U.S. Air Force F-16 Falcon, Gulf War ■ ROMEO: U.S. Air Force F-22 Raptor, contemporary ■ SIERRA: U.S. Navy Aircraft Carrier, contemporary ■ TANGO: M1A1 Abrams tank, Iraq War ■ UNIFORM: Arlington National Cemetery, Arlington, VA, contemporary ■ VICTOR: U.S. Marines, Iwo Jima, Japan, World War II ■ WHISKEY: U.S. Air Force A-10 Thunderbolts ("Warthogs"), Iraq War ■ X-RAY: Douglas DC-3/C-47, World War II ■ YANKEE: F-16 Falcons, contemporary ■ ZULU: F-14 Tomcat, Gulf War

An A-4 Skyhawk catches an arresting cable as it lands atop an aircraft carrier.

Bb BRAVO

A battalion of brave soldiers gets ready for battle.

CHARLIE **Cc**

A C-130 aircraft is loaded with cargo.

The Navy deploys a destroyer to help defend world peace.

Ee ECHO

Elite para-rescue forces egress from a C-130 Hercules.

FOXTROT Ff ◆

Foot soldiers wear bulletproof flak jackets.

Gg GOLF

Gunboats patrol upriver.

Huey helicopters transport soldiers.

oli INDIA

A United States Coast Guard icebreaker plows through icy channels.

JULIET Jj

Journalists travel in jeeps to report news from the front lines.

Kk KILO

Soldiers work with highly trained dogs in K-9 units.

LIMA LI

Marines, known as "leathernecks," make a beachhead landing.

Mm MIKE

Medical personnel work to save lives at mobile army surgical hospital (MASH) units.

Nn NOVEMBER

A Nuclear Class submarine navigates the North Sea.

OSCAR Oo

Before every flight the ordnance is loaded onto the planes.

ROMEO **Rr**

A Raptor refuels in midair.

Ss SIERRA

Sailors salute.

T-t TANGO

A tank thunders across the terrain.

UNIFORM **Uu**

Unidentified American soldiers lie in rest at the Tomb of the Unknowns.

VV VICTOR

Soldiers fight hard battles until they achieve victory.

A warthog pilot and a wingman make a landing approach.

Xx X-RAY

Rosie the Riveter provided extra support for the war effort.

"Off we go into the wild blue yonder, climbing high into the sun."—U.S. Air Force anthem

Zz ZULU

Zoom! A jet is launched off the flight deck.

AUTHOR'S NOTE

The military alphabet began as a way for service people to communicate with each other more clearly. When service people transfer information verbally, confusion between certain letters, such as the similar-sounding *B* and *D,* could bring disastrous results. By the time World War II began, the military alphabet was in use. In the chaos of war, where background noise made communication even more difficult, words were substituted for letters, and thus *A-B-C* became "Alpha-Bravo-Charlie." Using this alphabet, the *C* company in an army unit is called "Charlie company" over the airwaves. *F* becomes "Foxtrot" and *H* becomes "Hotel." There is no mistaking those official letter designations, and every recruit's first job is to memorize this new alphabet. It is their communication link and lifesaver as long as they serve in the military.

The international community later adopted this alphabet as the International Communications Alphabet (ICA), which is used by the airline industry worldwide. Given the complexity of moving aircraft through the skies—with each plane having its own letter and numerical designation—it is of utmost importance to be clear who is talking to whom.

The United States Navy has gone one step further by taking this alphabet and adapting it through the design of signal flags, so that each letter/name is given a color-coded shape. When ships run within visual sight of each other and want to maintain radio silence, they can use these flags to communicate. The Navy has also assigned additional definitions to the flags; for example, the flag for "Charlie" means "Yes," the flag for "November" means "No," and the flag for "Oscar" means "Man overboard."

Despite leaps in communications technology since the 1940s, when it comes down to the spoken word, clarity is of utmost importance to the military. "Alpha-Bravo-Charlie" will save many lives.